# Six
# Silly Foxes

# Six Silly Foxes

## Alex Moran
## Illustrated by Keith Baker

**Green Light Readers**
**Harcourt, Inc.**
San Diego    New York    London

First Green Light Readers edition 2000
*Green Light Readers* is a registered trademark of Harcourt, Inc.

Library of Congress Cataloging-in-Publication Data
Moran, Alex.
Six silly foxes/Alex Moran; illustrated by Keith Baker.
—1st Green Light Readers ed.
p. cm.
"Green Light Readers."
Summary: A family of foxes experiences a wide range of
emotions and needs over the course of a day.
[1. Foxes—Fiction. 2. Family life—Fiction.] I. Baker, Keith, 1953– ill. II. Title.
PZ7.M788193Si 2000
[E]—dc21 99-6813
ISBN 0-15-202560-X
ISBN 0-15-202566-9 (pb)


A C E G H F D B

A C E G H F D B (pb)

Printed in Mexico

We are six silly foxes—
Ellen, Max, and Greg.

We are six silly foxes—
Dixon, Beth, and Meg.

How can six silly foxes hop

on boxes filled with eggs?

We are six sad foxes. Look at that! Oh no!
We are six sad foxes, very sad. It is so.

How can six sad foxes fix an old banjo?

We are six hungry foxes, and it's time to eat.
We are six hungry foxes looking for a sweet.

How can six hungry foxes snack
on ice cream in the heat?

We are six mad foxes, as mad as mad can be.
We are six mad foxes. (Add it up—three and three.)

How can six mad foxes jump
into the next tree?

We are six happy foxes,
very happy, you can see.

We are six happy foxes.
You ask how that can be?

Silly or sad, hungry or mad,

we are all so very happy
in this mixed-up family!

# Meet the Illustrator

Keith Baker was a teacher before he went to art school. He writes and illustrates stories that he knows the children in his classes would have enjoyed. He says teaching was fun, but he really loves creating books. He hopes you enjoy reading them!